HENRY ALBUS

and the
Transformigation
Watch

HENRY ALBUS

and the Transformigation Watch

YAHYA ASHRAF

PARTRIDGE

To order additional copies of this book, contact
Partridge India
000 800 10062 62
orders.india@partridgepublishing.com

www.partridgepublishing.com/india

Contents

For my LOVELY Dad
and my SWEETEST Mom

Acknowledgment

First of all, this book for the reader because if you would not be there then this book would be also not be there. I would like to thank to my mother and father. For the critics.

I would like to thank, Racael Cruz, Gemma Ramos, POHAR Baruah, The editorial assessment, the book cover designing team, Mario Nelson, partridge publishing, penguin random house.

The Transformigation WATCH

Henry Albus was inward bound in an immense building. It was a gigantic university. It was a burgundy and azure patterned building. The university had a big pond. The vicinity not covered but the building had a gigantic sod with many flowers and swings. The gate was 15 meter away from the main edifice of the university. A gang of bullies were talking on the gateway. All they liked was to bully their juniors. Many people even left the university because of them. Even their director was afraid from them and didn't say anything to them!

Henry was an adult. It was his second year in the Milestone university. Milestone university was one of the best and most expensive university of Australia. He was the topper of his class. He belonged to a high end family. He had long brown hair and beautiful almond eyes. He had a long and pale face. He looked gorgeous.

Henry didn't liked the university because the bullies used to bully him. Thoughts use to come in his mind to kill them but he was afraid of going to prison. Once they took his precious thing. It was a Rolex watch of 5000$. He cried but they didn't give him. Life in the university was bad. The studies were also not nice there.

The principal and 'sirs' were very offensive. The worst thing was that the bullies were always in a bad temper. Mines no chance was left for a guy escaping from them. Noone use to like them.

Henry used to think that he is the biggest foe of them. He stood on the gate. He was standing there for a long time because he was waiting for the bullies to clear off. Someone kept his or her hand on Henry's shoulder. He was one of the teachers of the university. He used to teach him mathematics. His name was Jimmy Carter.

He was wearing a blue slim suit. He was a very good natured man.

'What are you waiting for Henry? Go inside.' Jimmy Snapped

'Oh! Sir, I am going inside, just waiting for my friends.' Henry said hastily

"I don't want any excuses Mr. Albus, go inside." Jimmy said sternly

Henry was surprised by this mood of Jimmy Sir and he went inside puzzled and frightened. Jimmy went in different direction and left. Henry was walking with heads down. He didn't wanted to face the bullies. He kept on walking without seeing anything around him. Out of the blue, someone kept his hand on shoulder. Henry was deadly terrified and startled. He was even afraid to see the damn face of that man. He looked back and took a sigh of relief.

"You have just given me heart attack." Henry sighed "But by heaven's sake you are not one of the bullies."

He was John Adams (Henry's best friend). John was the only person on whom Henry trusted the most. They both were famous in the whole university for their friendship. Henry use to share everything with John. John was a very good hearted boy. He was a boy who was not worried of anything, he use to enjoy his life.

They both were as silent as a sea. They didn't want to get in the bullies. John was also a boy who was always targeted by the bullies. And he was afraid of them.

Their heart was pounding with fear. Their heart came in their hands when the bullies started staring them. The situation became more complicated when the bullies blocked their way.

They both got scared and started to run from there. As they looked back, a bully stopped their way again.

'Hey! Where are you going?' One of the bullies said

'Hey! John and Henry you are now in our year' The bully laughed

'How?' John said surprisingly.

'These people have failed three times and now again they would have been failed and they have to study again, you know these people are born to fail.' Henry said boldly

Hearing these words the bullies were extremely irate. They held Henry's caller and threw him.

Henry fell on the road. They picked him up and slapped him. Henry couldn't bear his anger and he threw a stone on them. Henry knew that now he had to run.

He got up, took a cycle and started to cycle at the top momentum. The bullies also took their cycles and started to chase him.

John ran behind them. The bullies were shouting,

'Hey! Stop, you nugget.' Henry and the bullies came inside the wood. It was dark there. Henry ran and passed the old trees. The tire topples over the wreaked wood and fell on the damp expanse. He toppled over the woods and landed himself in the heart of the forest. The bullies had lost the faith of catching him but something happened and they tumbled over and landed directly in the heart of the woods. The bullied pretended to be fallen purposely to beat him.

One of the bullies went towards Henry and slapped him.

'Will you try to beat me?" said one bully mockingly.

They picked up the woods lying down on the ground and started beating him with it. Henry was crying, wailing and shouting but no one was there to help him.

Now Henry had to do something. He caught hold of a wood, snatched it and beat the bully who was beating him.

He got up and started running. They were trying to chase him but they failed as they were very clumsy and fat. Henry didn't realize that they had left him. He got tired and fell on the ground.

He saw in the sky and saw something. He spoke to himself.

"Is that a shooting star? No, how can shooting star can be seen at the time of afternoon? Ok! Then it can be a U.F.O!'

He thought to him 'have I gone barmy.'

The dot started becoming bigger and bigger. It started throwing something. It was a big pointed ice. Henry started running. He fell on the floor. He rolled and rolled and rolled.

He kept himself away from that pointed ice just for a moment. It fell on him. He was surprised to see that nothing much had happened to him. He caught an ice and took it out of the ground, like a plant. He started preparing himself like he was in a hammer throw competition. He targeted the U.F.O. Well a thing like U.F.O. He was befuddled to see that the ice was very light and with a bit force it went so high and hit the dot. The dot lost his control and it started falling like a disc.

It was becoming bigger and bigger. And yes it was an U.F.O. Henry had already gone bananas. He was not able to believe his eyes.

The U.F.O landed with simplicity. A big ramp came out. A small creature with green body, blue eyes, short height came out.

Without saying anything he gave Henry a translator. He held it. The alien started speaking.

"We are arresting you to do research on you.'

Henry was tongue – tied. He was unable to speak anything.

'We have come from Mars to do research on human body." The alien continued "And you are quiet useful to us" "Our space- ship has become bad."

"Someone threw an ice peak; do you know who threw it?"

"Err.....no...I....." Henry said.

Henry collected strength and said, 'You want a baseball'

"What's a baseball?"

"You wanna see it?" Henry answered

"Yes of course" the alien said eagerly. Henry went towards his bag and took out a baseball bat. He went towards him. He swung his bat and beat him on his face.

"What are you doing!" the alien said with fury.

"Oh! Sorry but this is only baseball" Henry said slay

"You beat me; I will slay you for this thing."

"We aliens don't deceive or say lie." He called some people from the U.F.O and ordered them to take Henry and put him in prison.

They took him inside the U.F.O then inside the prison. Henry was behind the bars. He was shouting but no one was hearing him. The U.F.O was the size of a hat from outside but from inside it was as big as a football field. There were more than thousands of aliens working with humans. They were just typing something silly on the computers. When they were pressing enter, the human sitting beside him was vanishing. They were typing-

#A false= Human v
#b= true= Human v
#c= mid= Human v
#Dm= calc= Human
#FS= Beside= Human me
#GS= WIRE RED= shoulder human= a*b/FS=? +dm=c
MD= memory= false
SD= memory= 2 years false
AS= Field (address) = GS
GS= Teleport to field
FF= Wire and block heads= remove= when= GS
RR= A, B, C, Dm, FS, GS, MD, SD, AS, FF, RR= Enter

The aliens put a helmet on the human which was having thousands of wires attached to it. When they press enter, the helmet falls on the ground and the human disappear. He was just able to see this when he found himself in a jail. He sat on the bed in the jail and started mooring over.

Henry went towards his bag and took out something. It was a small thing from which any lock can be opened. He went towards the lock and started opening it.

After hour's hard work, the lock opened. Henry was elated. He opened the door and came out. He hid from all the aliens and started making his way to the exit.

On his way, he found two people talking inside the door. Henry opened the door a bit and started hearing what they were saying.

The aliens stood there. One of them was that alien only with whom he met.

"This is the future of transformigation"

'What can it do?"

"You should ask what it cannot do."

The alien looked like a salesman and he was a selling a watch to the head of the aliens.

"From this watch you can turn into any liquid, anything or any gas" You can become fire, house, water, petrol and many other things.

"You can turn into a gas and fly in the sky." "You can turn into animals." "Whole world will touch you feet."

"You can run very fast by becoming plane partly."

"What it means?" asked the head of the alien.

"Mines, you will be having speed of an airplane but you will not look like an airplane, you will look like an alien."

"You can turn into anyone too"

"This thing is great!" "I want to buy it." "What is the cost?"

"70 heccon frest (70 million dollars)"

Henry thought to himself that this currency would be of their planet.

"I have to discuss it with my companions."

The head of the alien went out from the other door and the seller went in different room and Henry went in that room.

He picked up the watch and the guide and kept them in his bag. Then he went out of the U.F.O.

The U.F.O got up and soared in the sky. They didn't know that Henry was having 70 million dollars in his bag. Henry was very energized and curious buy his new thing.

He ran and came to his home. He took out the watch. The watch was of blue color. It had diamonds around it.

5 buttons were there on every side. Every button had a diamond.

Henry took out the guide book and started reading it. It had just one page. It was somehow like this.

Green buttoned diamond – Gas
Blue buttoned diamond – liquid
Red buttoned diamond - solid

Green buttoned diamond – partly anything
Orange buttoned diamond- Conversion in anything or anybody

You have to just press the button and think what you want to become as a result you will become till the time you want it and till the time battery is there.

For charging the watch you have to just keep it untouched for half an hour. The battery will last for 14 hours.

The name of the watch was the transformigation. Henry was very excited. His plan was to know take retribution with the bullies.

Now he has to not be afraid of anyone as he had the transformigation. He wore the watch. He didn't tell anyone in his house or someone else.

Henry's life had a big turn and now his life would be changed. He was extremely happy. He was not able to control his excitement for another day.

He was first time so excited to go to university as it was not one of the grey days which he had. Incessantly many ideas were coming in his mind to make the bullies a real donkey.

Indirectly, the bullies had brought a fortune for Henry because they only chased him and he was caught by the aliens.

Because of that only he is now having the power to do anything.

The story begins:

Henry Albus & the Transformigation watch

Henry Albus's mission

The day has come and now Albus's mission was to actually settle of scores. He took his bag and went out of the house.

"By mom, I am going to the university."

He took the university bus and came to the university. He became as powerful as undertaker by his watch.

He went on the way to the university. The bullies were standing there only.

'Hey, where are you going?'

'You beat us with baseball bat'

'Now we will beat you so much that you will be unable to go home.'

They took out their bats and beat him. Though he was having power of undertaker but he has been hurt a lot by this.

Henry fell on his knees. One person came in front and beat on his head.

'Auuu!" Henry fell on the floor. Tears rolled down his cheeks. A bully came towards him and beat on his head. They picked him up. They held his hand and made him an effigy.

One of the bullies came in front and started beating him with the bat. Henry was shouting with pain.

They left him. Henry fell on the floor. Now this was the time to use his powers but he was very impaired.

He was not having power to walk at all. He became gas and went home.

He was admitted to hospital. Days were passing. He took one month to recover.

1st week passed

2nd week passes

3rd week passed

In the fourth week he was fine and very nicely prepared to payback.

"I am not going to abide this." He got up from the bed, took his bag and went out of the house.

He reached the university. 'This is the last day for you' Henry said pointing one of the bullies.

'Oh hear him, what is he saying? I think his brain's nut bold have been loose after getting a nice pasting from us.'

The bullies were laughing. Henry went towards the bully and beat him.

'I will not leave you.'

Ken the bully swung his hand.

Henry held his hand, stared him for some time. Ken was shouting with pain. Then he left his hand with jerk. He left his hand and went away from there.

All the bullies were looking towards him.

In the class he crossed his limit. He became a gas and went in ken, the bully. He made him walk towards Jimmy Carter the teacher.

'Sir yesterday you beat me.'

'So,'

'Mines why you beat me!' said Ken shouting.

'Because you were disturbing your friends by making an airplane and throwing towards them and writing cheats and other things...'

'Youbeat me and now I will pummel you.'

'Be in your limits, you......'

Ken went towards him and slapped him.

'What have you done?'

Jimmy slapped him so forcefully that he fell on the floor. He did this because he was a teacher and Ken was misbehaving. 'You will be barred from this university.'

Henry went in another bully and he also made him do this. He did this with all the bullies. As a result they were expelled.

Henry was very happy with this. Now he was not poignant going to the university. His life was now radiant. But a sudden change has been in Henry. He use to know tease everyone.

He was completely changed. The only thing which didn't changed was his best friend, John.

Henry had changed completely. No one was happy with him.

Once he didn't want to study in the university and wanted to stay at home and he also didn't wanted to miss his work so he became the university and started shaking.

Everyone thought that earthquake has come. It was a holiday for a week.

Everyone kept on thinking that how the earthquake came because there was no news of earthquake was there in mass media.

Life was nice in the university. But he didn't know that what will happen after 3 years

After seven years

Henry's activities didn't changed. He was now no more a topper. John was not happy with him. John has called him many times to talk with him so that he can change his behavior but he never listened him.

Like every day, John called him today also. At last Henry agreed to meet him on '1st august'.

He called him in the forest.

'What happened, John?'

'I want to talk with you.'

'What you want to talk with me?'

'You are hiding something from me?'

'I am not hiding anything.'

'You are hiding.'

'I am not hiding anything.' Henry said coldly

'You are hiding, transformigation.'

Tom was shocked with the words John has spoken.

'How you knew about it?'

'Go in your reminiscence and try to remember what happened when the bullies were chasing you, I also ran behind them and I saw everything.'

Suddenly Henry was freeze with apprehension. He was flabbergasted.

'Remembered something, Henry.'

Henry held his hand. 'We have to run from here as fast as we can. More time we stay here, more we will be going in the pool of death.'

'What are you saying?'

'Don't ask, just run.'

They ran and ran and ran. Their speed was great. They passed

The old women's house, then the tree which looked like a woman, they passed the house of the dark witch and they went more deep and deep.

'John, the aliens said that they will be coming back after 7 years on 1st August.'

'But it's too late.' John pointed towards a star in the sky. It was an U.F.O.

Henry kept his hand on his forehead. "John, tomorrow we have to leave this continent.'

'Just once we get out from here.' Henry said

'Then of course we will be leaving to Jordon.' John said

'For now we have to go in another directions.' Henry said

'If in any emergency you need help so please give me a missed call.' Henry said.

They both went in another direction. After 10 or 12 minutes, Henry got a missed call. Henry became partly an airplane and went in that place.

7 aliens were there. The head of the aliens was same. One alien was holding John's neck.

'Oh! Look who has come.'

'We have come to take revenge.' Said the alien.

'We will kill you!' said the alien.

Henry became hulk of avengers. He held one alien's neck and threw him on the floor. He held other alien's neck and threw him towards an alien.

'leave john or this will happen with you.'

But something happened. Henry's watch's battery got discharged and he fell on the ground.

The aliens saw towards him and took John in the U.F.O.

'Leave him.'

'we will leave him, if you come on Mars.'

Henry was inarticulate. He cried in agony. His friends John had turned into ashes and is now with those aliens. He kept on crying in the forest. Suddenly he saw something on his lap. It was a 1000 year old envelope. It had a big round stamp stuck on it firmly. Henry opened it with a paper cutter which was in his bag. The envelope was empty. He threw the letter. After 2 or 3 hours an ox came there. He left his saliva on it. Suddenly something started coming on it. Henry picked it up and read it aloud.

"Henry Albus, we have taken your friend, We have just now kidnapped him but we can do much more. Give us our watch."

After he had read it, the letter turned into ashes and disappeared. He slept there for the whole night.

Next day:

Henry was sitting on the wall of his house. He was thinking about his friend. Cold air was blowing. Tears started rolling down his cheeks.

2nd day:

Henry was sitting whole day in the church. He spent his whole day over there, praying to Jesus Christ. Whenever you will see him, he would be crying. He opened his cupboard and took out anphotograph album.

He saw his friend's photo. He kept on gazing it for the whole day.

3rd day:

Henry was reading the paper and he got a big shock. The aliens has took 10 million people with them. And gave them warning to finish mankind.

They have told everything about HenryAlbus. Paper's headline

1- HenryAlbus shook the world.
2- Will this man be exiled.
3- Henry should be dead
4- Because of one person 10 million people will suffer plus their family.
5- He should be exiled from the world
6- He is a thief
7- Government say that Henry will be exiled from the world
8- Henry has to go to Mars
9- First time in the history
10- Henry is a convict

Henry was very sad by reading this all.

5th day:

Henry was sitting in his house where he got a letter.

From the government,

HenryAlbus, you are exiled from this world. You have to now go to Mars. We will arrest you till the time you don't sign on an important document. Then after that you will get 5 days to leave. Don't try to run because police is outside your house.

Henry was grief-stricken by this letter. Henry went out of the house and saw that whole vicinity was covered by police. Henry went to a police who looked like the head of everyone.

'I want pen and the document.'

The man gave him a pen and the document. Without reading the document, Henry signed it.

The police went away from there. Henry was exiled

From earth to 'ALIEN WORLD'

Henry packed his stuff and went to his mother's house. His mother gave him a ring which he has not wore till now.

He knocked the door. An old woman came out. She was crying. She hugged her child, Henry.

Henry also started crying.

'I know my boy has done nothing bad but you have done a mistake.'

'Henry, never be frightened, come with those people and never use your powers in vain.'

'world thinks that you are a scoundrel but for me you are a hero.'

Tears rolled down his cheeks.

'Mom you gave me 2 rings.'

'I have never wore them.'

'butnow today I will wear first ring and when I will return back, I will be wearing the second ring.'

Henry ran from there and went in a place where no one was.

He was in a forest. He was sitting on one of the rocks and mooring over his friend's kidnap. All of a sudden something came out.

It was a gigantic tin. It came towards Henry. Henry had decided what to do.

Then that tin turned into a man. He was having brown hair. He was having pale face.

His beautiful almond eyes were looking towards HenryAlbus.

Whereas Henry was seriously afraid.

'Sir don't be afraid, I will not harm you.'

'I am also like you' he said coldly.

'what do you mean.' Henry said

'can I tell you my story?' he asked.

They both sat that down on a rock.

'My name is James Bill' said the man.

'I am also having power like you.' Said bill

'I can also become gas, solid, liquid.' Bill said.

'You would be needing my help so please take me and my friends with you.' Said bill

Henry heard the story quietly.

'My friends are also having that power.' Said bill.

'Are you kidding' Henry said

From back a group of adolescents came out. It was a group of 2 people.

'they are my friends.' Said bill.

'We will stay with you and help you till the time we don't die.' James said.

Henry joined his hand and bent on his knees and said 'thanks everyone, it is my pleasure, I don't know how can I thank you.'

Tears rolled down from his cheeks. James went towards him and kept his hand on his shoulder.

'We will stay with you.' Said bill. 'You are now not alone.'

'Yes I am not alone now.' Henry said

'But first tell me what I can call you all.' Henry said.

'You can call me James' Bill said

A man with black hair, white face, blue eyes and brown moustache came in front.

'you can call me bounty.' the man said

'Henry but don't think that Bounty would have won something.' James joked.

They all laughed on this joke. Then the other came in front. The other one looked a little bad. He was having wrinkles on his face. He had white hair. His name was Fred

'we will leave tomorrow.' Fred said. They put a marquee in the forest and slept there.

Next day:

'Can anyone tell me how will we go to their world.' Henry said

'This work is of bounty' Fred said

'what do you mean?' asked Henry

'Bounty is genius.' James said

'hey! I have an idea.' Henry said

'we all can change into partly rocket.' Henry said

'No! we can't do this because everyone here don't have that power.' Bounty said

'Just you and Fredhave these power' Bounty said

'OK, we can think something else.'Henry said

'I have an idea.' Bounty said

'Henry I believe that you are the most powerful'

'Henry you have to change fully into a rocket and then we can sit in you and then we can go to our destination.'

'ok!' Henry said

'gracious, now let's go.'James said.

'No we can't leave just now' Henry said

'now what happened' Bounty said.

'We don't know in which planet we have to go.' Henry said

'Leave this work on me.' Bounty said "I can do this.' Bounty said

'We should just leave him alone and go to our tents' James said

Bounty sat down on a stone and started concentrating. They all went to their tent.

After an hour they went back to Bounty.

'So what you have thought Fred.' Henry said

'Henry there are many planets in the world.' Bounty said

'From which we know just 9.' He said

'I can say that their resident is not in these planets.' He said

'They live in a natural satellite of Mars and we have to go there, But there they call this satellite as mars only.' He said

'Bounty can help you, he knows everything about this world.' Fred said

'Ok! So we are going just now.' Henry said

Henry changed into a rocket. They sat inside him. Henry flew in the air and landed on Mars after a month. From Mars they saw it's natural Satellite. Then they took a rest and after a week they **reached there!!!**

A new member

There world was 1000 years further from us. Henry and his other companies changed into aliens.

'Let's go.' Henry said

'No, we can't go just know.' James said

'But why?' 'we can't stay here without Ella.'

'she is the person who knows everything about this world and she can open any lock in this world.'

'we will not be able to survive here without Ella.' Bill continued

'ok! But where is she.' 'Here I am guys.'

A young girl with long brown hair, white face and red lips came smiling and shaking her hand. She was wearing a black shining legging and a white top.

She hugged James and her other friends.

They talked a lot. She was now Henry's friend. Henry, Ella, Bounty, James and Fred were going to bring the people back. The story is going to begin of these warriors. Now what will happen? Will the survive the attacks.

Author talk:

Hi readers,

I am Yahya Ashraf. I like to talk with my readers. I love you as you are my reader. I will talk with you in every chapter of this book. I would like to share with you about this books fact. You know this story was never a success for me. I gave this book to many traditional publishers but they rejected me. I was feeling opposite of this☺. I lost the hopes of my book getting published. Some publishers accepted me. They were trade publishers but they took money for publishing. Olympia publisher who accepted me took 2500$ for publishing my book. My previous book's publisher took $1500 for publishing and it was a self – publishing company. I always wanted my second book to be publish by trade publishers. But this dream was never completed. I kept Olympia publishers a side. I thought if no one will publish my book then Olympia will publish. I got rejection letters from 12 publishers. If you are interested in reading them then mail me at yashrafjamescook@gmail.com. You can give me direct message on twitter. My profiles name is yahyaashraf110. After two months I mailed Olympia again but I didn't have any response. I mailed them again. But they told that My name was deleted from the data sheet. I was sad again☹. I didn't touched my book again for the next month. But one day I got a phone from partridge(my older book's publisher)☎ . Poharbaurah who was my publishing service associate told me that the package which I bought had a contract for another book also🖹. As a result this book was published by partridge. In the next author talk I will tell you about my previous book.

Some information

They changed into gas and flew into the air. They were following Ella. To reach the city they need to travel 3000 km more which is very much. Ella was flying the fastest of them. She was flying in the speed of 1000km/hr.

Whereas Henry (2nd fastest) was flying at the speed of 900km/hr. They were unable to catch her speed. Henry held both the hands and suddenly shot like a rocket at the seed of 2000km/hr!!!!! He was enjoy the chilly fresh air of the atmosphere which was passing through his face. It was the best moment of his life. He didn't realized that he was flying in such a high speed and he was lost. Fred and James also took the speed to catch him. Ella and bounty were told to go to their destination. Ella and Bounty had reached to the city. Henry was completely engaged in his thoughts.

"Ella, do you see me, I am flying faster than you."

"Fred c'mon let's enjoy."

"Let's get faster"

Henry became more faster and he was flying at maximum speed of 2783.22kmph.

Everything was done now. He was now going into the pool of death.

"Ella, according to my data we have covered 3500 km. But we have not reached our destination."

"Hey, why you all are not answering"

He got down and saw that he was in a sandy place. It was a forlorn place. Sandy harsh winds were blowing like anything. No one was there. He kept on seeing here and there. He didn't realized where he was. For some time he felt like he had lost his memory. He knew that that place was not lonely. He felt someone was there. Suddenly he looked back. He saw an alien. His hands were having a blue virtual shield. Henry looked in the front to run but there also that man appeared. He looked left then right but he was appearing in all the direction.

"Who are you" Henry said

"I think you know Nalmart." That man Said coldly

"Who is this?" Henry asked with fear

"He is the king of this planet and you know he got many **people** who is working as a slave in our palace. I think 10 million people.

"Shut up! Just tell what you want." Henry said crushing his teeth."

"I want you. My master want you. Whole mars want you. Give me the watch. When you will come with us to the palace then we will first put you in inside a hot sand. We will take you out and then make you walk on fire and when it will be your last date then we will put you in a room. Where we will put a device on you from which you will not die for 1 day. In that one day we will kill you thousands of time. We will fire you with 100 bullets. Then we will cut your head. After that we will cut you in 5600 small parts. Then we will leave in between of thousands of birds and insects."

Henry turned into fireman. He made a fire ball and threw it towards him. He became a small dangerous rocket and flew towards him. Henry banged with him. There was loud bang. Everything was covered with fire. Henry's clothes were torn. He was covered with black powder. That alien got up. Henry changed into a gigantic airplane partly. He held his hand and flew and soared in the air. It started becoming difficult to breathe. Henry left his hand. That man fell on the ground. He was badly injured. He held his caller.

"Tell me from where you have come. Tell me your name. Tell me."

Out of the blue came Fred and James.

"Hey Henry, How are you." Fred said.

"I am fine. This man was trying to attack on me."

"Attack on you? Are you fine?." James questioned

"Yaeh, I am fine but I don't think so he is fine."

"C'mon let's go." Fred said

"He will also come with us."

"No! He can't come with us."

Henry went closer to James and Fred and whispered something. They nodded their head and that man went with them. They reached to their destination.

"Hey, Henry don't you understand. Are you crazy? We can also go on your speed but we didn't because we are afraid from the thing you have passed right now. You have gone out of your brain." Ella shouted

"I am sorry but this turned out to be good for us in a way. Errrrrrr... Yaeh not very much.....but yaeh."

Everyone was looking towards Henry.

'Hey! Guys why are you looking me like this."

"And how this accident is good for us?" Ella said coldly

Henry pulled the man in the mantelpiece and said "I got this man, he was trying to....kill me but........"

Henry told everything what that man told him.

"But how you know that the man knows everything we should know for our mission." "He is just a type of... employ." Ella said sternly

"And that to not a high esteemed position so that the devil can tell him everything" Fred interrupted

"Err...I didn't thought of this" Henry said to himself

"You said something, Henry" Ella said

"NO"

"So tell us, how you know."

"Hmm. I figured it out."

"But this will be proofed only if I ask him."

"C'mon everyone, spread out, I need some place."

They formed a big circle. In the middle was a man sitting on a wooden chair and Henry looking sternly towards that man. He was carrying a big steel rod.

"C'mon tell me your name."

That person didn't answer. Henry asked again. He warned him that if he will not tell then he is dead. He beat the rod on the man's shoulder. The man shouted with pain. He beat again on other point. He kept on beating but the man didn't say anything. But the man said something.

"Beat me."

That man was badly injured. Blood was coming out like anything. Henry kept on beating. He picked him up by his caller and said

"You will regret."

Henry went out of the room.

"I want a meeting right now" Soon they were in a big room. There was long table which was actually Fred who has turned into a table. Everyone had a paper and a pen with them.

"This man who is there in the room, knows everything but he is not telling."

"But I have an idea."

"Fred you will turn into money."

"Money?" Fred said

"Listen me carefully. When you will turn into money then we will offer him that money so that he can tell us everything. Then when he has told us everything, Fred will turn back in himself and I will turn into a machinegun and we will shoot him."

"That's a good a idea" Ella said

"We will execute it tomorrow."

They went to sleep. Next morning they gathered in the room. Fred has transferred into 100,000 million Frest (Frest is the currency of mars). He was in a big bag. Henry was holding it. They went in the room.

He placed the money in front of that man. He took the money.

"My name is Kane Bradman. I am a soldier in Nalmart Army. Nalmart is the king of this world. He is the most powerful man in this universe. Every Marsiansss don't have power like you. It is the king and the people who are connected with him have the power. But they can just turn into solid, liquid and gas. They cannot turn into anything or partly anything. But Nalmart has another substantial power. Whatever he touches, he becomes that. But he can use this power only for saving his powers. Nalmart wanted to become more powerful. So he got the best scientist of Mars, Earth, Venus, Neptune and lugomanchester planet. He got Raneegd, Albert Einstein, Fellicocks, Geondero, mander, moutrested respectively from each planet. They all were dead people. Since we were 1000 years further then Earth, we are able to make dead people alive but it can be done just ones. We also had the power to mix anything. And we build a thing from which brains can be mixed. He took these people's brain and mixed it. A super intelligent brain was made. He put that brain in a common Marsians. That man was named hellicon. He can use 15% of his brain. That man went on a project from which anyone can change into solid, liquid, gas, anything or partly anything. He needed people so they went on earth. There they captured many people. The watch was made after 2 months. After that Nalmart had to give him lots of money and own it. But first they need to take the people's memory(the people who worked with hellicon) and then drop them back to earth. But that time you saw them. They were afraid so they kidnapped you and thought to kill you but you stole the watch. Hellicon can't make it again because he saw you when you were trying to steal the watch. He ran after you but at that time the U.F.O started flying but he didn't noticed that and jumped from the U.F.O and he was dead. The watch is with you now. From that time Nalmart became bad to the people of the earth. He kidnapped these people. If you give him the watch then he will leave everyone but you will die. You will die badly. And these people who are helping you will also die. Better, give the watch, and surrender."

"But why Nalmart was behaving so well." James asked

"Nalmart is good. He is not bad like you all. He just wants powers. He has not harmed anyone. But he will kill you and those people because he had loss of billions of frest. Go, if you want to save them."

Kane took a sheet of paper and a pencil and drew something. "If you see this kind ■ of figure then remember that it is the sign of frest."

Kane took the suitcase. Abruptly, Fred changed back.

"Hey you!" Kane said

Kane started changing into liquid but at the right time Henry has changed into a machine gun and he has fired Kane a hundred times. He was dead. Henry took his hood and went out of the place.

"Hey Henry, where are you going?" Ella shouted

"To the palace." Henry answered

"Henry, have you gone bananas. You will be dead." Fred warned

"So, for this disgusting watch, I will put life of 10 million people in danger. No! I cannot do this." Henry shouted

"But we have not made any plan, how we will go." Bounty said

"Just I am going. Not we. I cannot put your life in danger just for my help."

"But what about the plan." James said hastily

"We have a plan."

"Which plan?" James questioned

"The plan which we made right now."

"We didn't made any plan."

"I made in my brain."

"And what is that." Bounty asked

"It is go and die."

"You all go, on earth. Save earth."

Henry went towards Fred. He kept his hand on his shoulder and said

"Take care of them."

Henry wore his hood and went somewhere. His friends kept on shouting. They stopped him but he didn't. They even cried.

Author talk:

Hi,

Good morning/Good evening/Good night/ Happy birthday(if you have)

I am the author of this book. In this author talk, I will tell you about my previous book, James Cook. James Cook was never been published easily. It all happened on a teacher's meeting. My English teacher praised me and said that I will go high if I start writing. But others teachers did many complains about me. But I was fascinated about what my English teacher said. I started writing a book in my scrapbook then in my diary. The first name which I kept was The mummy then Robert then Robert lee and Lord Saten. Then finally James Cook. I wrote it in many things. Someone told me that there is a publishing house nearby and I went on the search. I went in printing press and he told me everything about publishing. I got to know that I have to first type it and I did it. I wrote the whole book of 226 pages. I started trying to find publishers on Google. I typed publishers and on the top of the list was an ad of a publisher. It was notion press. I mailed him. He accepted to publisher my book but he wanted 1 day to analyze my book and I knew that he will reject it. So I found a new publisher. It was partridge. On that day I got a phone call from Indianapolis. Reseal Cruz told me everything about publishing and I was fascinated by being published by a self publishing company of Random House. I also got mail from Notion Press that they accepted my book. I was confused now but I choosed partridge. The money was paid and I came in the publishing world but I had to face many difficulties on this journey. In the next author talk I will tell you about my journey. It was one of the most difficult journey

Of my life. I faced many problems. But I got my goals.

The attack

Down the street, Henry went. It was pitch dark. Henry didn't knew the way but he moved. He kept on moving without safe. He was just thinking that if he die than those people would be save. He went to a teleport stop.

Glossary- teleport stop- A stop where you have to just stand and think where you want to go. Pay the money and you would be there in a second to your destination.

He paid the money and came to that place. It was gigantic building. It was as large as Canada. Henry was like an ant in front of that building. He stood there and kept on gazing the building. He changed back into his original form. He was back into human. He went towards the door. It was fishy to see that no one was standing there. But the aliens were invisible. They were now visible when Henry reached towards them. The aliens saw them and Henry's picture was available on the wall beside him. He was shocked to see this. Under that it was written "HenryAlbus, VVIP" Henry went inside. Every alien was seeing towards him. Henry felt like a celebrity for some instance and then remembered he was a guilty. He went straight to the court. Nalmart was sitting on a peculiar chair. It was a chair made with water for his comfort. There were thousands of buttons made with diamonds. Nalmart was not like a normal alien. He looked like a normal human being. He had long black glorious hair. He had a bright face. He had long height. He wore a black suit.

"HenryAlbus, I didn't thought you were going to come."

He called a person from the room behind and said him to bring a kambrono device.

Glossary- Kambrono- A device from which a person can be alive in any type of situation for a day.

"Henry, we are going to put this device on you then we will kill you thousands of time."

"It will start by cutting your neck!"

Henry took out his hat and placed it in the feats of Nalmart. He bent on his knees and bowed. Nalmart put the kambrono device on his neck. He took an axe and placed it on his neck and then Crash!!!!!!!

"Don't dare to this also with my friend."

Fred was holding nalmart's hand and Ella, Bounty and James were fighting with the other members of the court. Henry was saved. Henry gotup, he changed into fire and threw a fire ball on Nalmart. Nalmart raised high in the air and fell on his seat. Henry changed into forgono and through all the spines on him.

Glossary- Forgono- A man who throws giant spines made up with ice.

Henry threw those spines on Nalmart. They went straight to Nalmart's chest. Ella blackmailed an alien and told him to take them to the place where those people are kept.

"Henry, Fred, Bounty everyone come, we have to save those people."

They all ran after that man. Many aliens tried to stop them but they weren't able to stop them. They reached a place. It was a dungeon. The prison was not like a normal one of the earth. Instead of having bars they had a wall made up of iron. There was something called an oxygen tunnel where Oxygen can come in and go out. There was even a kitchen for them. They had beverage store also in their room which uses to give them drinks, juices, shakes, water, many types of food etc. There was a miniature thing placed on the wall. The man told them that if you on it for a minute then the room will be at the temperature of 5 C! You can also control the temperature. They moved towards the wall. Something started scanning them. The wall spoke "Strangers, Kill them"

A giant monster came out of the wall.

"Why didn't you told it before to us." Ella shouted on that man.

"AHHH! Best of Luck!" That man spoke and ran from there

"A coward one." Henry said

Henry changed into liquid. All his friends changed into gas.

Henry changed into a ghost and went inside the monster. He started controlling his body but the monster was very heavy and it was very difficult for Henry to control him as a result the monster threw him out of him. Henry fell on the land. Ella was trying to stop him but the alien picked her up and threw her. Fred and Jameswere trying to tackle him but they failed. Other hand Bounty was trying to find out how the monster can be stopped.

Henry changed fully into dragon. He first took his friends and kept them in a save place. He went towards the monster. The monster looked completely blank about the dragon. Henry threw a fire on the monster. The monster was burnt. Henry then changed into a big diamond. He rose into the air and fell on the monster's chest. Something black started spurting out from his chest. It was black blood. The monster fell on the floor with a thump!

"Ahhh!At last."

Henry went towards his friends.

"I did it."

All his friends went towards him and hugged him.

"But it is not possible for us to again go there, because I found out that if we go again then again that ogre will come, so it's better we have a better plan." Bounty said

"Ok! We will come back with a better plan."
James said

"Yeah" Fred said

"Ok! We will come back." Henry said

"Yaeh" Ella said

They all held their hand and came to their
house. So we have to first make the plan.

They sat together in the meeting room and
started discussing.

"Nalmart is very powerful, we can't lose him."
James said

"If he is very powerful then why he didn't try
to kill me at that moment." Henry argued

"There is a reason. I have lived on this planet
for a week but I really don't know about Nalmart.
But something I know. Nalmart will not kill you
easily. He will first try killing us, your family and
your friends. He will snatch whatever you love,
then he will kill you. So we know that it would be
very difficult. Nalmart is very powerful." Ella said

"Every person in this group has a specialty.
Henry can change partly into anything which no
one in this group can do. Fred can change into
anything which just Henry knows how to do.
Bounty is very brainy. Ella is very fast in speed
and I am good in fighting." James said

"So if we use these things nicely against
Nalmart then I think we will succeed." James said

"But this is the question, how will we do
that?" Bounty asked

"Very easily." Bounty and Henry said

"I have a plan." Bounty said

"And what is that." Fred asked

"By attacking his palace."

"Are you out of your senses? It would be very dangerous!" Ella shouted

"Calm down, I know what Bounty wants to say. I and James are good in fighting so we will go together to the palace. We would be wearing a device so that we are connected. Bounty is very brainy so first someone from our group will follow his instructions and hack the camera of the palace. Through this Bounty can see us and he can also control who see me and James. So there would be no chance of us being caught. We will be in the costume of an alien so maybe the guards don't catch us. If he catches us then we will take help of bounty and enter the prison. Once we have entered their, we will hold each other's hand and come here. Bounty is working on the teleportmachine. Once the teleport machine is created those people will go on earth. We will stay here and plan to kill Nalmart."

"Very nice plan, Henry!" Ella exclaimed

"Brilliant, Bounty." Fred said

"Yaeh Fred is correct." James said

"Thank my friends." Bounty and Henry said together.

"Leave Bounty and James alone. They have to hack." Henry instructed

Author talk:

Hi, nice to meet you again. I promised you that I will tell you about my previous book. My book James Cook had lots of problems while getting published. I was assigned by partridge. I got a call from Racael Cruze. He explained me everything about getting published by partridge. First I thought it would be very easy. But it turned out it's opposite.

It was very difficult getting published. The first obstacle was that my book was not finished. They kept on asking for my book but it was not finished. Then my PSA suggested me to first make the cover. I accepted this. They gave me a website called think stock. From there I had toselect some pictures for my book cover. But I didn't liked any so I bought the package from which they will make the book in the way I want. They made the picture. 2 weeks had past and my book's cover was ready.

I gave my PSA the book. And then I got a message which changed everything. She told me that some of my book's characters were similar to the characters of this book****. I would not tell you the book's name. I was shocked because I knew that I have not cheated it from that book. Then I messaged her again. She told me that my content was not similar, the book cover was similar to a part of that book's movie.

I took a sigh of relief. But she told me that I have to change the book cover and the content also needs to be checked. But the results were in my favor. Now I just needed to change the cover. A new cover was made and my book was published. After that also many problems were there but those I will tell you in my next author talk. ByBy! Have a nice day. And remember you can follow me on twitter at yahyaashraf110. Happy reading! But I would say proudly that Partridge is a brilliant publisher. Everyone interested in publishing then please publish with partridge. Believe me, it's a brilliant publisher.

The going of James and Henry

The day passed by no one getting out of their room. They were fully exhausted. But they woke at one time. All of them gathered in the lobby to execute the plan.

"So we are here." James said

"Bounty, have you hacked it?" Henry asked

"No, we are trying out best but maybe we fail." Bounty answered in sadness "It is really very difficult to hack the camera of 30s century. At last I am a civilian of 20th century. It is asking for some codes but now I am now trying to program it in my way. But I am not getting the proper software to do it."

"So please hurry up." Ella said

Bounty and James was sitting on a white sofa. They all were stuck to a laptop. A green screen was there. A red thing was showing loading percentage.

"We did it." bounty shouted "We have done what we wanted, now just programming which is really very easily."

"That's good news." Ella congratulated

"Now it's gonna be easy." Fred said

"Yaeh, it is our first step to success."

The programming was done and the hack was successful. Now no one can see what's going on through cameras. Henry's companions can only see what's going on in that damn palace.

The hack was successful and now it was the time for James and Henry to go in that palace.

"The hack is done now when you are going to go to the palace." Ella asked Henry and James

"After a month."

"What after a month, are you crazy?" Ella exclaimed

"Yaeh, after a month." Henry said "because we have to practice lots of skills to do it."

"Today, we both are going to leave this home and go in a silent place and practice there." James explained "Now everything is on your shoulder."

"Does everyone know about it?" Ella asked

"They don't know, but you are going to tell." James said

They picked up there back and went out of the place. They also didn't know where they need to go but they just knew that they will try to be in a place where there is peace.

On they went on their journey.

"So what's gonna happen, now?" Ella asked no one "They both have went, we have to survive without them for a month."

"They have not gone for a month; they have gone for a year or half." Fred added

"What!." Ella said shockingly

"Let's go to our room." Bounty suggested

One by one they all went to their room. They were not able to sleep they were lost in their own thoughts. They all were tensed on the decision of Henry and James. They were so angry with them that they can even kill them. Tears rolled down from their cheeks in the memory of them as they all have become strong friends. They were thinking if Nalmart kills them. If Nalmart attacks them. If Nalmart is making a plan to finish them. One more problem which they were thinking of that if Nalmart has forced them to go there and they didn't wanted to tell them. The problem which everyone was thinking of that if something wrong happens to them. They all were not able to sleep so they went out of their room. Accidently they came together in 1 room and at 1 time.

"Why you all are here." Ella asked Fred and bounty

"We can ask same question to you also." They both answered

They talked there for an hour. There life was not good. They didn't had any sleep. 1 month had passed and everyone was thinking about James and Henry. They were very tensed. The second moth passed with the increase in tense and less sleep. On 1st august they were in the Hall and were talking about their life on Earth. Their mother, father and sister.

Suddenly something fell. The roof of the house broke. Smash!! Smash!!!Smash!!! Everything above them fell. The 3 cried and shouted. They were blank. They were not able to get what is happening. A small figure fell on the ground. He was wearing a black hood which was smaller than his head. He was chocking the things which have fallen on him like a mountain. Small pieces of woods, cements, dust, stones and other things have fallen on him. Suddenly he came out of the mountain of dust and said "I was knocking the door for an hour and had to come from the roof. Next time please open it."

The 3 were not able to get what's happening and who is that alien. Ella collected the strength and asked "Who are you."

"Yaeh I thought you are going to ask me this that's why I got this." That alien answered. He took a trodden paper from his pocket which was kept roughly in his pocket. He started reading it.

"I am the alien from lord Nalmart's Court. I am here to find Henry Albus. I am saying again give me Henry Albus, I will give you life and the people also. I am saying proudly that I will kill you. I am very powerful. I am from Nalmart's court and I am here to get Albus. If you don't give us Henry then you are coming with us to the prison. There you will be burnt and death will be in your palms so better giving us Albus. I am saying last time. You will be safe. Give Henry or I will throw you in the prison. What will happen to you there, no one knows. Give me Henry." That alien read the paper "So how was my speech, I wrote it whole night. I didn't slept. For this speech. My acting was faboulous?, sometime I think that I should be an actor"

He kept on praising himself and his acting. Ella was bored with it and she changed into fire and threw a fireball on him. Ella, Fred and Bounty changed into gas, solid and liquid respectively. Fred changed into a drum and beat that alien on his face. Ella had gone in him and she was burning him from inside. Bounty had changed into acid and he was also burning him. With pain that man was shouting.

"Wait a moment" said the alien

He threw everyone out of the house. He changed into anesthesia and injected everyone. In a blink they had fainted. He took all of them to their palace and kept them in the prison.

Author talk:

Hello nice to meet you again. Guess if you are fine and you are not ill. I pray to god for your fastest recovery if you are ill. And if you have any problem in your life then they will be solved soon. May God give you all success in your life. I was always inspired by J.K Rowling. I have read all her books and I always wish if I were J.K Rowling. Her books, Harry potter are great and I also want my books to be as success as hers. I want to become an author and I am. Let's get out of this topic. As you know I am a very young author and I have written 2 books till now. I am also writing the third book. I can tell you the story but I can't tell you in this book. You can always give me mail at yashrafjamescook@.gmail.com you can also send me DM at yahyaashraf110 and you can follows me also at this locat-

Ion on twitter. You can visit my website www.cookjames.com. I love writing that's why I write. I know at some moments you are getting bored in this book but I think you will forgiveme because I am very small. I am just 11. Goodbye! Happy reading.

In the prison

"What the hell." Ella said

"These people have put us in the prison!" Fred shouted

Bounty went near the prison and shouted "Take us out from here. You will repay for this. Take us out from here."

"Take us out." Fred shouted

"Takes us out : He repeated again

Suddenly someone thumped his or her iron rod on the wall and told them to be quiet or it would be not nice for them. But They shouted and challenged them.

Suddenly the iron door opened with a screech. An alien came in the room. Bounty went towards him and held his collar and said him to leave. He told him that if he doesn't leave then he will be dead. Bounty gave a signal to Fred and he changed into gas. He was now in Bounty's pocket. Bounty knew that the people of mars are completely new to guns. Though they are in 30th century but they don't know anything about guns because here everyone lives in peace. No one has ever harmed anyone so they don't need any type of ammunition.

Bounty again warned him to leave them but he just nodded his head side by side.

"Ok! Then you have to face it."

Bounty took out the gun from his pocket and put it directly on his forehead. Suddenly bounty realized that there were no bullets in the revolver. He spoke quietly to Fred that he has not changed into bullets. Fred's answer tensed bounty more. He told him that in a glimpse something is going to happen and he has to change in bullets and gun at that moment only.

The alien found something fishy and said "You can't do this with me. Nothing will happen with it. I will shout if you do something.'

Bounty tightly made his fist and punched him tightly on his right cheeks. The alien fell on the floor with blood coming out from cheeks. As fast as possible, Fred turned back in human and changed into bullets in gun.

This happened in a short lap of 2 seconds. You can say in a glimpse. Bounty went towards the alien and picked him up.

"Now you will make us get out from here."

He held his neck and put him against the wall. Bounty knew that he will not die by bullets but if he will shoot him with one bullet then he would be injured badly and probably he would think that if I shoot him second bullet then he will die, it would be his end. Bounty held his neck and said that if he will not help them find everything about the palace then it would be his end.

"This bullet will kill you in two laps. So I am shooting the first one and if you don't take us out then I will shoot the second one."

Suddenly there was a shout. Banggg!! The alien was lying on the floor. Blood was coming out from his head. At one chance everyone thought he is dead but he wasn't, he was just badly injured.

"Now will you help us?" Bounty said "or you need the other and the last dose."

That aliens hand has changed into a green flag and it was waving. This means that he would help them but he will take lots of time to recover. They hid the alien beneath the bed. Bounty was trying to find out how he will recover fast.

1st day:

Very bad condition. Blood coming out from his head.

2nd day:

Blood was coming out from his head but they have taken a portion of bounty's cloth and wrapped it.

3rd day

Blood is not coming out and he is better but someone comes in the prison. He comes at 11.59 so the rest on the fourth day.

4th day:

The man has come in. He is thinking if something is fishy. He goes to have a better look beneath the bed. Everyone is scared. Their heart come in their hand. He sees everything. But at the right moment Fred has changed into a gun (with bullets) and bounty was holding it. He again blackmails him with the example of that alien. He gets ready to help them and they live together.

5th day:

The alien is recovering fast. He can now speak and eat. The other alien is bring medicines and good food from the palace so he is recovering fast.

6th day:

The alien is recovering very fast. The other is now their friends and they are living happily.

7th day:

The alien has recovered 70 percent.

11th day

He had recovered fully. He is also their friend and ready to help them. They are making plans.

Author talk:

Sorry no author talk but you can always mail me at
<u>yashrafjamescook@gmail.com</u>
and follow me at yahyaAshraf110 (twitter)

Secrets of the palace

The two aliens Geonda and Meonga were workers in the palace. They were good hearted person so they agreed to stay with them and try to defeat Nalmart. Geonda was in the army and Meonga was the Prison keeper. Meonga knew more than Geonda. Meonga took the lead and went to explain them everything.

He started with a corridor which was having prisons on every step.

"This is the prison room; here the captives of war are kept. Here is another strip of prison rooms where the people are kept who are unable to pay their debuts. In the next strip thieves are kept."

"Where are the criminals kept?" Bounty questioned

"My friend, the criminals are hanged." he answered

Meonga pointed towards a place where the aliens were getting hanged. It was frightening prospect for them.

"Meonga, I should not ask but we also have done many crimes so we will be also hanged." Ella asked scarily

"Yaeh, you will be hanged but if Nalmart get to know about it." Meonga answered "And I guess..... he know...."

"But how you got to know." Geonda asked

"Ahhh! I just figured it out from his face....."

The 3 were frozen to death. They swallowed their saliva. Sweat started coming out from their forehead.

"Don't be afraid my friend, Nalmart would have seen us and we also would be hanged." Geonda answered

"Don't be afraid, he will not be able to see you through the cameras as they are hacked by me." Bounty answered

They further went on their journey. They saw a giant wooden door.

"This the treasury room." Meonga said "The room behind this is Nalmart's treasury. And let me tell you that Nalmart's treasury is more than the money for the citizens. Since Nalmart can't see us then we can open it." The wooden door opened. Their eyes were pinned by the glamour of gold. Gold coins were all over the room. The room was as big as a 10 story house. Money was all around the room. The room was filled with it.

"You can take how much you want. They would be useful later."

Geonda gave them lots of bags. They filled the bag fully. They have got 72k feast. Geonda went to the nearest teleport station in the palace and teleported the bags to their home.

Next we go to the x room. In this room the foods were kept.

"You can take the preserved food. They would be also very useful for you."

They took the foods and teleported to their home.

"Now we have to go too far for the next room so we are using teleporting machine. I know that you all have never went by a teleporting machine but this would be your first experience. Remember that this machine will take you to whatever place you want in mars."

They reached to the teleporting area. Many teleporting machines were kept. They were getting used by aliens. They would go, press button and stand in the machine. The machine would then vanish and come back after 5 seconds. A long line was there on every machine. The aliens were not able to get who they are because they were wearing alien's costume which was provided to them by Meonga and Geonda.

They had to wait in the line for a 10 minutes. Now it was their turn. Zillions and trillions of buttons were placed on it. Weird names were written on it. On the entrance of the machine was a big table. On it you have to press the section where you have to go. Geonda pressed

The palace section. The door opened. They entered the machine. The machine was having lots of other sections in it. There was a search button too. Henry wrote "Nalmart's palace" in it. Suddenly a big screen came in front of them. He pressed Nalmart's Palace section button. The buttons changed. Geonda pressed the chemical room button. Suddenly all the buttons vanished.

The machine took a jerk. It started speaking "Thank you, have a great ride."

The machine started rotating. It started rotating faster and faster. The machine was getting smaller and smaller too! The passengers were shouting and wailing.

"It is going crush us, stop it." Ella shouted "Stop it."

The machine was getting more smaller. It had now reached their head. The machine became more smaller. It passed by their heads. It didn't did any harm to them. They were shocked to see this. The machine was now till their waist and it vanished.

"It would have reached to their station." Geonda told them

"But where are we!" Fred asked

It was fully dark around them. They were not able to see anyone. It was jet dark. Suddenly, the path on which they were standing, started shaking. It kept on shaking for a minute. After it had stopped, light came out from the front.

"Move." Meonga urged

They moved and they saw that they were in the chemical room. It was a magic for them. They kept on talking about their experience with each other. Geonda and Meonga were bored with this and said "Guys, I think we should move. In front of them was nothing.

"Where we should move? Where is the door to the chemical room?" Fred asked

"You are standing on it my friend." Meonga said

Fred quickly stepped back. He saw a wooden door. It was the door to the basement. All the attention was towards it. Meonga went there. He opened the door. From his expressions we can tell that it was very difficult to open it. They had to jump in it. They jumped at once. They shouted as they passed by the giant tunnel and reached to the end of the room. It was dark there. Meonga went towards the switch and switched it on. They saw that they were in a room which was filled with chemicals.

"Here you go."

Author talk:

No author talk. Remember you can always follow me at yahyasharaf110. By! Happy reading.

The Chemical room and the news

Meonga opened the giant door. A type of bad smell was filled in the room. The next second their hands were on their mouth. It was a disgusting smell. They had not stepped inside also when Meonga stopped him. He gave them transparent gloves to wear. They were made up of a very fringy material. Next he gave them a mouth mask. On first look, it appeared a small mouth size cloth but by turning it we got, it was a mouth covering mask.

"It is a very impotent thing, without it you may die because of the smell here." Meonga warned

They went inside. The room was filled with thousands of variety of chemicals. But none was similar to those of Earth. Some chemicals were so strong that they would finish the Earth. They were of peculiar colors and shapes too. Some were fully transparent. Some were like a sun, like a moon, like a man, like a house, like a planet, like ammos etc. It was very strange to see this. Bounty, who was a scientist, was lost in his own thoughts. He was thinking about how much science have increased, science was now at different level. He thought to write all these in a book name 3030 of earth or a book named 'let's go to mars". Bounty was not able to control himself and asked about the shapes of the chemicals. "I accepted this question from you." Meonga answered He went towards a chemical, which was having a moon shape. He opened the lid with lots of force. As he opened it, a blue small screen came out. It was have two options. "Virtual""Hologram"

He clicked on the virtual option. Suddenly they came in space. They were flying. In front of them was the most beautiful planet, Earth. They can see the sun and many other planets. Stars were above their head. They realized that they were flying on moon. The moon didn't looked nice because it was having its craters and holes in it.

"By this option, astronauts can go in the space in seconds."

After saying these words, he clicked his fingers three times and the screen appeared again. The screen was flying, so Meonga had a strenuous job to press hologram button. He pressed it. As he pressed, they reached back to the room and moon's 3d figure appeared in front of them.

"This is used to teach the students." Meonga explained

Everyone was taken aback by these things.

"This was a very important room, so I showed you. You all can go and see the other chemicals but be fast, we have to cover much. They went and saw everything. There were many kinds of chemicals. All most everything was there. Ella stood near the showcase and was staring on one chemical for a long time. It was a liquid chemical in transparent color. A monster was made on it. She went towards Meonga and asked him that if she can have it. Meonga's answer was No, a big no. Ella started saying please and melting him by her words.

Meonga can't see her tears and talked to Geonda about this. After a long talk, Meonga agreed.

"Ok! You can have it but just one spoon, it would be enough."

He gave her that chemical but just a teaspoon. Ella went towards Fred and Bounty and said "We can use this chemical to kill the monster outside the prison."

They went out of the room and the dungeon. They had moved a step when an alien came running towards them.

"Meonga! Run......nalmart....knows....Run...." He said

They shared their looks and ran as fast as they could.

Author talk!

Sorry no author talk. But remember that you can always follow me at yashraf110 on twitter or mail me at yashrafjamescook@gmail.com

The death!!

They ran as fast as they could. The 3 kept on asking questions but Meonga and Geonda would just say "keep on running". They were running towards the teleporting machine. In few minutes they were standing beside a big line. They just went and pushed everyone. They used their powers to throw them away. Meonga quickly pressed the outer Mars button then the north and 2225 house number. They were frozen to death when they saw Nalmart. He was running and coming towards them. 5 soldiers were back of him who were carrying dangerous items. Nalmart said "They can't run away". Their heart was pounding with fear. Nalmartwas getting closer and the door was being shut slowly. They all were frustrated by the pace of the door. Nalmart's nose havejust reached to the door when it had met with each other. The machine took a jerk and started rotating. When it had reached their head, it stopped. It was a statue.

"What I was afraid of, that only happened." Meonga and gonad said scarily

"What has happed! Tell us." The five questioned

"You will get to know."

Suddenly the machine was back in its original position. It took a jerk and opened. In front of them Nalmart was standing and looking at them sternly. The five shoulders have placed their armors and machines on them. They were getting Goosebumps and were frozen to death. They swallowed their dribble and came out of the machine. The machine's door closed. They were handcuffed and those handcuffs were not normal. Those would tell if you were thinking to run away. If they detect this then the men would be informed and those handcuffs would get more powerful. They would start getting hot and burn your skin till the time you leave the thought of running. They went silently to the place those people were taking them. They came in a giant ground. It was thrice bigger then a international football field. Many soldiers and aliens were there. Nearly 1000 aliens. They were clapping and cheering. Some were saying Meonga and Geonda betrayers. Tears started rolling down their cheeks. They got the same feeling when a prisoner gets when he is getting hanged. They were taken to a place where they would keep their head and Nalmart would cut it. It was something made a material which was not available on Earth (at least no one has found it). It had a big cut on the thing. If someone will keep his or her head on it then the cut would become deep and would be the size of the person's. Nalmart gets hold of Bounty's hand and took him to the place. He forced him to place his hand on that material. His friends were not able to see it and they turned their face. They were trying to stop their breathe and do suicide. Nalmart took the modern axe which tells if he is dead full or not. He first placed it on his neck and made and large. He started murmuring something in his ears. He was moving the axe around his neck and was trying to find the right location. That bloody axe helped him find the right location from which he will die at ones and will get more hurt. It was just in the middle of his neck. Suddenly he picked up the axe. He rose it as much as he can and then put it just in the middle of his neck with all his force and then..............

Crash!!

Author talk:

I guess this would be the saddest and the most breathtaking chapter. You will be sad by the thought of losing all your friends but at least read this chapter. I know you will now not like to read this chapter full. And yes let me remind you, this chapter is not finished. I am just saying to read the full chapter. If you will read without thinking that your friends, Bounty, Ella and Fred are dying. Just read it full without a stop.

Crash!!. Smoke was all around the ground. No one was able to see anything. The smoke cleared. Henry was holding Nalmart's hand!!!

"Stay away from my friends or this would be your end." Henry said to Nalmart. He picked him and punched on his face tightly. He flew in the sky and crashed 5 feet away on the ground. Suddenly in the scene, James came. He was flying and coming.

"James, take a good hold of Nalmart." Henry ordered

James flew towards Nalmart.

"Chief! Call the army." Nalmart ordered to the chief

Henry went towards his friends. They were clapping and cheering for Henry and James. Henry came and made a very powerful shield around them. Through which they cannot be harmed. In few minutes they heard stamping noises and they saw that Monsters, aliens, peculiar animals etc were marching towards them to kill them.

"James, Come here." Henry shouted

James was busy beating Nalmart but by hearing his voice he came in their shield. Ella pointed towards Meonga and Geonda who have been hid in a corner and were crying and sobbing. They were looking very innocent. Some aliens were coming towards them to kill Meonga and Geonda.

"Go! Save them." Ella requested "They have helped us a lot."

'Ella, have you gone nuts! Why will I save them?" Henry argued

"Just go and save them." Ella said

"No! I won't save an alien in my life, No I won't." Henry fought

They kept on arguing. Henry said "no" and the 4 said "go save them".

"Are you peopling mad, I am not going to save them!" Henry said

Ella was not able to do it and she slapped tightly on Henry's cheek

"Go! Save them." Ella said in harsh voice

Henry kept his hand on his red cheeks and broke the shield. He rose in the air and went towards them. He caught a alien and converted his hand into a chainsaw machine. He sliced his neck with it. The other aliens ran from there seeing this. He picked up Meonga and Geonda and threw them in their shield. They were now in the shield their friends were.

It was getting more danger. Henry was busy killing aliens when a monster broke their shield. Henry saw it and at right moment. He moved his fingers and threw something towards the alien. The alien turned into ashes. But then another monster came in. James changed his hand in chainsaw and cut him from his waist. Henry and James charmed something from which lots of orange color gigantic bars were around them. They were levitating in the air. They were 2 feet above the ground. Whenever any alien came to kill them, those bars would contract and then extract. When It extract it gave out light from which those aliens would go far and crash on the ground. It was more powerful than the other shield.

Henry was now surrounded by aliens. Aliens and monsters were everywhere. They were looking like they are just going to eat him. They were of green color and were carrying a baseball bat. It was not a baseball bat but it looked like. It was as big as an 11 year old boy and as fat as a television.

Henry took a step back and continuously focused on them. He got an idea to make them afraid. He would kill 4-5 aliens and 2-3 monsters. The other would get afraid and run away. He went towards an alien and threw him. While he was flying in the air, Henry took a high jump and landed on his stomach. He took the other one and locked his hands. His hands were under henry's hands and he broke it. He lay behind the other alien. He took the other alien and kept him on his knees. He raised his knees and the alien flew a bit. At right moment he kicked on his hips and flew very high. When he landed, the other aliens flew high. Henry took the opportunity and killed all of them. The other aliens were afraid and went one step back.

Henry ran towards a monster. He kept his feats on his knees and jumped in the air. He did air summersault and landed on their baseball bat. It broke. He landed on the ground with an ease. The monster ran towards him. Henry just punched him tightly and his fac buried in the sand. He kept his leg on his buried face an waited for him to die. This he did with the other monster too. He took a hold of other monster(because they were not afraid). He took quick movements of his arm and it started turning blue. Then he held that monster's caller and punched him. That monster went very high in the sky and landed with a thump. He was dead badly. By seeing this, other aliens and monsters got more afraid. Henry took again quick movements and his arm started turning blue.

"My arm has turned blue" Henry warned "I will run north and anyone can be killed by it."

He turned back and started running. Everyone got aside and Henry kept on running and he fell.

The arm's power had become very less but it had effect on the ground. All the soil, concrete, dust etc were like a pile on Henry.

He was able to hear some sounds which were of his friends. The army took the opportunity and went towards Henry. They picked him up and started beating him brutally. James was not able to see this, he broke the shield and went to save them. He beat all the aliens and made them away from Henry. Henry and James did a thing from which there was a bomb and all the aliens were lying back on the ground.

They held their hands and flew from there. They took all their friends including Meonga and Geonda and went from there. They went to the nearest teleporting station and teleported to their place.

Author talk:

Hi! Nice to meet you. 2 times author talk because this chapter was an interesting one. Now we are moving towards the end slowly. The end has nearly come. As you know, Nalmart would turn back and try to kill them. The story is getting finished. This would be the second author talk because the other chapters are very hurting. This would be maybe the last author talk and there would be the next in the last chapter. By! Happy reading.

James and Henry, the storyteller

They all went in the teleporting machine and teleported to their house. "At last "Home sweet home" I love our house. We were very sad being alone. I and James use to cry every day. We use to cry every day. We use to sit beside the sea shore and glance over the sea. We use to miss all of you. It was very difficult for us to live without you all". He went towards the desk and saw something. Henry was aback to see lots of money and food in the house. He questioned to them about the food and the money. In the answer they told the whole story which has happened with them. After hearing the story henry and James went towards Meonga and Geonda. They hugged him tightly. They said them sorry and they both went out of the house. They sat on the rock which was kept behind him. They started talking about everything when Ella called them.

"You have to do your dinner." Ella said

They all sat on the dinner table and started talking about the things which they have missed.

"James and Henry, Please tell us about your training."

"We went in a forest, a dense forest." Tom explained "It was a very dense forest. We went straight to the heart of the forest. We wanted to be in silence. We changed into human forms and we didn't use our watches for at least a week. It was a very tough training. We use to keep on touching and kicking trees till the time they don't fall. After the continuous training we actually did it. In a week, we had become so strong that by giving 5 punch and 5 kicks we can fall a tree. But this wasn't enough. We wanted a trick to do these things. We kept on thinking of tricks. And one night, in James's dream, Jesus Christ came. He told him that we 5 are doing a very good job and he will help us for it."

Tell more, what happened after that." Ella insisted

"Yes, yes tell more, anyone of you, please tell." They all insisted

"James, go for it." Henry whispered to James

"Yaeh! Wait a second, I am continuing" James said

"Jesus Christ came in my dream and told me exactly that he is very happy with our work and he will help us for it" James told them

"Oh! Please don't stop, continue." Fred said

"I suddenly woke up, something was glittering in the forest." James continued "So, I went there. I found a bright box. It was very bright and I thought if something important was there in it. I took it to our tent. Next morning when Henry woke, I told him everything what happened that night. Henry was as curious as I was to open the box but we both were frightened also. Henry placed the box on a tall tree's branch and kept on thinking what can be there in the box. I was getting frustrated by this and I opened it. Henry shouted on me and tried me to stop from opening it. But I opened it."

"Oh! Please don't stop at the boiling point of the story." Geonda said

"Yes, please carry on." Meonga persisted

"For heaven's sake, don't stop." Bounty said

"After this Henry will continue."

"I went towards James and shouted on him. I shouted that what would happen if there would be bomb, what would happen if we would die after opening it, are you out of your senses." Henry told them "I even slapped him for this thing. I was really worried for him. Yes, I gave him abuses, I slapped him, I shouted on him but I said him sorry for a thousand time."

"Please tell us about what the heck was there in the damn box." Fred interrupted

The 5 were listening the story very carefully with their hands on their cheeks and their elbows resting on the table. James was checking if Henry was going right.

"Be patient, I am telling." Henry snapped "When the box opened a model of an angel popped out. It was having a diamond stuck on its wand. We took out the diamond. As James put his fingers at the bottom a big bright screen appeared. On it all the tricks were written. We have to first put a finger on the bottom of the tree with all the force then on any of the branch twice. Then a punch. The tree would fall. There were a quite large number of tricks for aliens and even hypnotizing them."

"There were 650 tricks for aliens." James interrupted

"Yes maybe because you were counting it." Henry said "James wrote all the tricks in his notepad. We practiced all the tricks on animals, aliens, tees and other things. All were successful and we learnt all of them. After James had written everything and we have learnt everything, the diamond vanished. We were awestruck to see that thousands of animals, zombies, aliens were coming towards them. It was a test for us. If a lion would come, we would press two of our fingers on his heart and then on his shoulder, he would die. Like this many tricks were there and we used them successfully for killing them. But there were tricks for the transformigation watch and we learnt them also. In a day the war was finished. All the animals, zombies, aliens were dead. And we had won it."

"Oh! So brave and powerful you both our." Geonda praised

"What happened after that."

"After that..." James said "After that we took a rest and went to sleep. Jesus Christ came again. But this time in Henry's dream. He told him that they have passed the test and now they know everything. They should burn the notebook and return back the ground of Nalmart's palace. There, your friends are in danger. Go fast. So Henry told me everything and we burnt the diary. We flew to the ground of Nalmart's place and we found Bounty getting killed."

"Jesus Christ had helped us a lot and we would be always thankful to him." Henry and James said

"We are now very powerful and now we are ready to face Nalmart." Henry said

"Bounty, have you made the machine?" Henry asked

"Nearly, made it." Bounty answered

"Good!" Henry replied

"I think we should revise the plan." Bounty suggested

"Yes we should." James said

They all sat down again and started talking about the plan.

Author talk:

Hi! Nice to meet you again. Very pleased to tell you that we are reaching towards the end. Are you exited but please don't read the end straight away. Wait for it patiently. I study in Cambridge school and it is

A good one. I know every student in his or her life hate a teacher. Similarly I use to also hate a teacher in my old school. But if you are talking about friends then are like a medicine. Friends are better than teachers. We can learn things online also but can't have are medicines which are our friends online. Best Friends always stand with us. Like my stood with me. I want to tell that make friends a lot. Friends are very good. And later you will see it. By! By happy reading.

The restaurant

"It's simple and easy. I and James would go to the prison. We will try to kill the monster and seek in. We will simply try to go to the teleporting machine and teleport to this place. Bounty has made 2 machines. One of them can finish mars and the other can make us fly. Mines, we will give it to all the 10 million people and they can easily fly. They can be in the space. In the space also we fly and we will reach to earth. After we have reached to earth, we all will come back and kill Nalmart. We can then go back to Earth."

"Any questions."

There was silence for a minute in the room when Fred broke it.

"Can it happen that we kill Nalmart at that moment when we are saving them…"

"We can do this but this will lead to danger. If Nalmart kills us before we kill him?"

"So, Meonga and Geonda, tell us where is the nearest teleporting machine."

"Oh! It is near the ground which is too far from the prison." Meonga told them

"So, we have to keep a teleporting machine, there?" James asked

"I guess, But it is not easy to do this." Meonga answered

"We have to simply put the teleporting machine where ever we want?"

Henry asked Meonga

"I guess...we..." Meonga answered

"Ok! I am going to steal a machine and keep it there."

Everyone tried to stop him but he didn't. Henry went on street. Down the street there were many aliens walking around. The streets were same as those of London. They were very clean. There were just shops and restaurants. Henry wandered what was the food given. So he went in one of the restaurants.

It was gigantic piece of apple. The apple was as big as a 5 storey house. It was in bright red color. And a leaf was put above it. The leaf was too gigantic in size but not as big as the apple. On the leaf something was carved with cream. "The apple"

It was most truly the name of the restaurant. Henry was in a form of an alien so no one was able to see something uncharacteristic about him.

He went towards the restaurant. As he went near, two aliens appeared suddenly. They examined his face and vanished. Henry was puzzled. He went more closer and the apple restaurant opened apart. He came inside. Many aliens were sitting on tables and chair. Henry found a chair for him and sat down. Something in red color was put on it. He pressed it. Suddenly a waiter appeared

"What do you want sir!" the waiter asked

"Hmmm, the best dish of here."

"Ok! Your order for the gelepon jecks is confirmed, it will reach you within a minute."

The waiter went from there when Henry called him

"Yes sir, what else you want."

"The food will reach me in 1 minute but that's too le….."

"Yes sir I know that but Gelepon Jecks takes lot of time to be made."

Henry was shocked by this.

"Can you tell me, what this red thingis." He pointed towards the red thing and said

"Oh! There's a pair for each. Every table has a unique waiter. For this table, I am. When you press it then the pair which is kept in the kitchen starts ringing. When it starts ringing then I have to keep my hand on it and I will reach to the other pair. Which is here. This can work even if you are on other planet and someone else is on other planet."

"Oh! That's amazing!" Henry exclaimed "Can I have one."

"You can have it but it costs a millions fest."

"I will give you." Henry said "Bring this when I have finished eating."

Suddenly the waiter vanished and a big apple came in front of him. Henry kept his hand on the apple and it some spoons and knife came. The apple opened apart and It was a plate now. It was having a desert. It was of yellow color and many fruits were mixed it. Henry tasted it and it was awesome. It tasted somewhat like the north American dish Quebec.

After it has finished, the plate vanished and a bill was kept. Even the pair of machine was also kept. The bill was of 1,005,000 fest. Henry tried to stand up but he wasn't. Till the time he would not keep the money on the bill, he can't get up. Henry tried a lot but he failed. Then he tried to use some tricks. He tapped on the arm of the chairs and it broke it. Henry got, took the thing and ran out of the restaurant. The waiter ran behind him. Henry tapped on his heart and his shoulder, he died. All the staff of the restaurant was running after him. He ran and ran. He tried to get to the nearest teleporting station. He reached there. A big line was outside the machine. He threw everyone out of the line. One of the alien ran towards him to punch him. He punched him but henry stopped his hand. He held his hand and beat on his face. That man fell on the ground. Henry opened the machine and came inside. It was shutting slowly but one of the staff member came inside. He was a powerful man. Henry pressed his house button. But that person held his hand and stopped him. Henry kicked him on his ass. He fell on the ground. The person rose up again. Henry tried to beat him again but this time that person did something that his left hand was locked. It was not able to move at all. Henry didn't stopped for a long. He pressed his three fingers on his stomach then on his heart. The last stage was to press on his heart again. As he was going to press it, the man stopped him. He blocked his right leg. Henry held his neck and ticked once He was dead. Henry opened the door. He threw him out of the machine.

"Mad person but nice try." He murmured to himself.

He pressed his house button and reached there. Ella helped him to do his leg and hand proper again. It was fine again. She just shake his hand and it was fine again. They all go to sleep. They had decided that next morning, they would execute the plan.

Author talk:

Hi! Nice to meet you again. No author talk but you can always mail me at yashrafjamescook@gmail.com or follow me at yahyashraf110.

The execution of the plan

"We have got no time, I and James are going."

"Ella, when I will call you then you have to tap this thing." James explained

They were wearing something from which they can talk to each other. They were carrying a bag which had lots of dangerous things. They both wore a t-shirt and a jeans. A black jeans for camouflaging in the dark. And a black t-shirt too. He wore a hunter's cap which had a torch attached in it. Their shirts and jeans had a hidden materials inside it.

They left the home when Ella called them. She ran towards them and gave them a purple looking chemical. (remember something)

"You can use this to kill the monster." Ella said "Simply fall in on his head."

Henry took it and they went hiding to the teleporting machine. Henry was transformed in an alien but James had to wear the costume. They came to the nearest teleporting machine. They pressed Nalmart's palace button and went inside. The machine started rotating. In 2 or 3 seconds everything was dark. They started walking and came in front of the palace. Henry knew that the guard will recognize James so he thought to kill him.

He went towards the guard. The guard appeared suddenly and started scanning him. When his scan was completed and something fishy was detected, James just punched him. Henry took the charge of the other guard and punched him too. They both were dead. They entered in the palace. Lots of aliens were moving around. They all were wearing a black hood and a big clot rapped on their body. It appeared as it was compulsory for them to wear the hoods. Their cap had a peculiar symbol. It was two snakes intersecting. The two snakes had their tongue out. On the right snake's tongue N was written. On its tail A was written. On the left Snake's tongue I was written. On its tail m was written. On the top where the snakes made a V, a, was written. Downwards where they made a V, r was written. In the middle where the snakes intersected, T was written. On every second the color of the snake was changing. Sometime it was becoming blue, green, black, brown. After all the colors had finished just Nalmart was written. All the aliens were looking at them. They figured out that James was not a real alien. But they didn't cared about this.

They both headed towards the nearest teleporting machine which was behind the document room. There was a big line of aliens there. They stopped there for at least half an hour waiting for their chance to come and it came. But they didn't knew where the prison was. So they called Meonga.

"Hey, we are in the teleporting machine, which button to press. Thousands of them are there." James asked Meonga

"Yaeh, try to find prison corner." Meonga answered

They started searching for the prison corner. After a long hunt they found it at the most bottom.

"Meonga, we have found it."

"Ok! Now tell me the names." Meonga ordered

"As you wish." James answered

"Henry, please say the name, Meonga want to hear them." James said

"Dungeon prison, prison, betrayers, for the dead......."

"Ok! Now please tell the prisons which are under dungeon prison corner."

"Henry, Meonga wants to know the contents under dungeon prison." James said

"Yaeh!" Henry answered "It has only two, 1 is prison and the other is by my name."

"So please tap your name prison." Meonga answered

James cut the phone and pressed the button. The machine started rotating and they reached to their destination. Breathing there was not at all easy. It was 100 meter down in earth but some devices were put through which oxygen is made. They went towards the prison. It was a very big prison. It was as big as an island!

The monster appeared. It was much stronger and bigger than that of the army.

They started climbing on him but that monster held him and threw him on the ground. Henry landed with a thump. James did a high jump and ticked on his heart and shoulders. They monster didn't died but lost his balance. Henry took the chance and flew in the air. He rose high and kicked on his face powerfully. The monster fell on the ground. They quickly opened the chemical bottle. But the monster rose again. He moved his hand and henry crashed on the wall. He picked up James and threw him away. They both stood up.

They were severally injured. Henry changed his hand into blue and punched him on his stomach. The monster fell on the ground. Henry opened the chemical and fell it on his head. The door opened automatically. The 10 million people were sitting in groups and crying. There were kids, men, women, parents, grandfather and grandmothers.

As they saw someone they became scared. Henry went in and on their torches. They were now able to see that it was Henry Albus who is here to save them. Everyone started clapping.

They came and started hugging him. They started shaking their hands. Some of them tears rolled down. They both also started crying.

Henry heard someone shouting his name. Henry looked back and saw John Adams. He ran towards him and hugged him. They talked for a long time.

James ordered them to sit in a circle.

"So my dear friends, we are here to save you." James said

As he said this, everyone started shouting and clapping and cheering.

James took out that gadget which henry has brought from the restaurant and said

"All you have to do is just keep your hands on it. If you keep on the hand of other's then also it will work but that person's hand should be on the gadget or interconnected. So go on and keep your hand."

Everyone ran and kept their hands. Henry called Ella and told her to tap it. Ella tapped it and they all came to their house including Henry and James. 10 million people were now in their small house or hut maybe. It was impossible for them to be in the house. The house had broken due to this humongous amount of people. They were now on mars and they need to go because anytime the aliens may come and kill them.

Author talk:

Good, you have come till here. The end is coming. It is very near so keep on reading. Will henry make it? This thing is written at the back of the book. So to get the answer read the book. This book don't resembles that

How will Henry bring them back to earth, this book tells that will Henry be able to kill Nalmart and bring those people back. And yes I will always say, this book can make a difference. Yes I know this book can't make a difference in the society but it can make in your life. Now you will ask how? Let me tell you. Whenever I use to be very tensed, I use to simply go and read Roald dhal books. They us to cool down my mind and make a difference in my life. In some ways I use to do what the writers wants me to do. I get tense free and enjoy my life again. So, I can say this book will make a difference in your tensed life. Remember, you can always mail me at yashrafjamescook@ gmail.com or follow me at yahyashraf110.

By! By happy reading.

2ⁿᵈ last chapter

"So, guys we should better hurry up or everything will be finished." James suggested

"C'mon everyone, we gotta hurry." James said

"Yes! James is beyond doubtfactual." Henry said "C'mon keep your hands, we are going."

"C'mon what the heck your are waiting for." Ella urged

"Hey! Henry we aren't going through this machine, we need the flying machine." Bounty said

"Oh! Sorry so please wear them." Henry said

"Henry, I would take at least 5 hours." Bounty said

Henry said "Take your time but try to be faster."

Bounty took out a very heavy jacket which he was wearing. It was a yellow jacket with strips all over. It was not a type of a jacket. It didn't had arms. It had strips which you have to wear tightly for the best protection. It had a type of small screen put on the heart of the jacket. It was a small screen. You have to type where you have to go. Bounty typed Earth(north America). After he had typed it, the screen started loading. After few minutes, on the screen done appeared.

Next he took out 2 giant green machine. It was green in color. Bounty placed his jacket on its top. After it was placed, bounty called 6 of the volunteers.

"Please help me keep this machine on this jackets. The volunteers helped him to keep the machine on the top of that machine on which the jacket was placed. It was now like a sandwich. Bounty pressed it and a small screen came. He typed 10 million.

It took 1 hour and the jackets started multiplying. There were 10 million of them.

"Please everyone wear it tightly, or you might fall and die." Bounty said

Everyone started wearing them. Ella went towards Meonga and Geonda. They were standing and looking to the people and how happy they were. Seeing their face anyone can tell that they were said. Anytime they can burst into tears.

Ella kept her hand Meonga and Geonda.

"I can see that you are crying."

"Oh! No I am not crying." Geonda said

Ella rubbed her finger on their eyes and showed them a drop of tears.

"So, what is this." Ella said

"These are the tears of happiness." Geonda lied

"I know you are sad, tell me what is it that is making you sad." Ella said

"Ella, don't go." Geonda said

"I will come soon. Do not worry." Ella said wiping their tears

Suddenly they burst into tears. They were saying her to stop.

"Ok! I am not going, I will be here with you."

"Oh! Thank you Ella, we will be always grateful for this." Meonga said

"I am just coming." Ella said

She went towards Henry. He was standing in a corner and talking with John.

"Henry, I want to talk with you." Ella said

"John, can you please excuse." Ella requested

"Yes." John answered

"Henry, I am not going with you. I will stay with Meonga and Geonda. They are alone." Ella said

Before Henry said anything Ella said "Please I don't want to hear anything."

After saying this, Ella went from there. After an hour everyone was ready to go. They said by to Ella and Meonga and Geonda. They flew in the air and vanished. In a day or 2 they reached to the Earth and their place.

Henry left the other people and went to his mother's house. As he reached there, thousands of media and people came out of his small house. Everyone wanted to have a look at him. Henry didn't wanted to talk to them but his mother forced him to go.

"Ok! I will tell you what happened there." Henry said "I, Ella, Fred, bounty, James went to save those people. Nalmart who was the king of Mars was a good person. He had never harmed anyone but he would harm me for my deeds. He wanted to kill me. We were living in a small house which was in outer Mars. A man named Kane Came to kill me but instead we killed him. He told us that if I will not die than those people. will also be never left. I became very emotional on this and thought to go and surrender. Without listening anyone I went there. Nalmart was just going to kill me when My friends saved me. Then we decided that we should make a plan. According to the plan I and James needed to go to save those people. Bounty needed to make a thing from which anyone can fly. One more machine from which Nalmart can be dead. But bounty made one more machine. A machine from which anything can be multiplied. To kill Nalmart we needed practice so we both went to a forest for practice. After we returned back I saw that my friends were imprisoned and they were going to die. We both saved them from dying.

There was a great war in which we won and came back. We executed the plan and we are here. But yes, let me remind you that Nalmart is still not dead and we will go back to kill him and come back again. Anything else you want to know then Please go to Fred, Bounty or……"

After saying this Henry went inside. The reporters and his fans asked lots of questions but Henry didn't answered any. He went inside and sat on the sofa.

"Mom do you remember what I said when I was going." Henry asked his mother.

"Yes I remember." His mom said

She took out a small diamond ring which Henry gave her when he was going. She wore it. Henry was in tears. He took out his ring which was in his pocket and wore it. They both hugged each other.

Next morning:

Newspaper headlines:

Our superman returns

10 million people with him

3 more friends with him

Where is Ella?

Fred said that Ella won't come

They will return back today

Will the government accept him?

The 3 came out and left the earth in the morning. It took them again 2 days to reach. They came to their house.

"Ella! We have come." Henry shouted

But he was shocked to see. Ella was fallen on the floor and Meonga and Geonda were lying on a table. Everything was ruined. Ella's blood was all over the floor. They ran towards Ella.

"Ella what has happened to you, get up." James said crying.

Everyone was crying.

"Henry please control yourself, she is dead."

They went towards Meonga and Geonda. They all were crying on their death. Some were sitting beside Ella and some were beside Meonga and Geonda.

Henry went out and sat on the rock. He was gazing in the sky and thinking about Meonga, Geonda and Ella.

Author talk:

I am really very sorry. Now the next chapter is the last chapter. I am again very sorry for the death of Ella, Meonga and Geonda. You know what I thought first? I thought that in the end Henry would marry Ella but I didn't. I liked this story better. Hold your hands, close your eyes because the last chapter is breathtaking. After that you have a chapter which is not important for you to read but you can read for fun but I am afraid, you should read it. If you would not read it than how will you read the next part of the book. But let me tell you something first. When I will grow than I will write this book again with more engaging style because I am a young author. I am just of 11 years and just going to turn 12. My birthday is on 1st august. Today I have came on periscope so you can follow me on periscope too. yahyaahraf110 is the id for twitter

And periscope so please don't forget to follow me and remember you can always mail me at yashrafjamescook@gmail.com. Best of luck for the next day and yes Happy reading. No author talk for the next chapter.

By!BY!

The last chapter

Henry had went far away from that place. He was sitting on a rock and gazing towards the beauty of the sea. He was thinking over his friends' s death. He sat there for at least a hour. Suddenly he remembered something. He went in flashback and started remembering what had happened. He rewind and remembered that their blood was purely fresh. Their body was not stinking at all.

"This means that............ nalmart had....... not................" Henry spoke to himself. This means that Nalmart had just killed them. Henry stood up and ran across the street. He ran and fast as he could. He had changed into a gas. He reached there in a second. What he was afraid of, that only happened. All his friends were dead leaving James who stood beside Fred and crying. Suddenly someone threw something. Henry ran to save him. James fell on his hands.

"James, what has happened to you."

James was badly injured. Blood was coming out from his head. He was breathing fast. The thing which someone threw went straight in his neck. He was crying silently.

"Henry, henry" James repeated "Nalmart......
heee.....willlll...............lll.......u...rnnnn."

"James, who did this." Henry asked "Please
tell me, I will finish him."

"Henry....nalmaa....GO......hee will kll u.....
rnnnnn"

After saying this James head fell and he was
dead. Henry shouted "Naaaaalmaaart I would
killlll you"

After saying these words, Henry went to the
nearest teleporting machine and teleported to
Nalmart's palace. He killed every alien who came
in his way. Anyone who would come in his way, he
would simply kill him. Without saying anything, he
went to the top of the building. It was raining cats
and dogs. It was midnight. Winds were shouting.
He stood there with all the anger in his eyes.

His hair and jackets were flying so high that
sometime the jacket would touch his hair. He was
wearing a black inner with a smart brown jacket
on the top. He had a blue jeans. He wore finest
quality shoes.

He was looking gorgeous. Due to rain, he was
fully wet. He stood in the Middle.

He shouted "Nalmart, if you have courage
then come here." "I would finish you."

The rain started getting more dense. Nalmart
appeared there in a second. Henry was standing
in one corner and Nalmart on other. There was
going to be a war. It would be the most dangerous
war of the world. On one corner super powerful

Nalmart and on the next corner the person who has lost his friends, a person who has transformigation watch, a person who is the hero of Earth.

Nalmart ran towards henry. He got hold of his waist. He put him air and threw him on the ground. Nalmart ran towards henry. He kicked on his stomach. Henry bounced and landed again. Nalmart picked him up from his caller and punched very tightly on his face. He punched him again and again.

Then he punched him so tightly that henry flew in the air and landed with a thump. Nalmart made a fireball in his hand and threw it on him. The ball burst. Smoke was everywhere. When the smoke settled, henry was not there. Nalmart started looking here and there

Henry wasn't there. Someone knocked on Nalmart's back. He turned back. As he turned back henry clouted very tightly on his face. Henry ticked on his heart right and left and then on his shoulder but nothing much happened. He just lost his balance.

Henry and nalmart made a fire ball and ice ball respectively. Their fire ball met with each other and there was a bang. They both were injured.

They both stood up and ran towards each other. Henry held his neck, tangled him on his chest, did a long jump and threw him in the air. When he was landing, Henry rose and placed his leg on his chest. Nalmart bounced once and landed again. Henry held his neck and tried to kill him while nalmart was trying to remove his hand from his hand.

But Nalmart removed his hand. Henry came over him and started beating him. He ticked on his stomach and then on his knees. After he did this, Nalmart's body started turning into blue. He rose in the air and landed with a thump. Henry picked him up and went near the balcony.

He picked him up. Through this nalmart was paralyzed. Henry took a mike from the palace. It was actually not a normal one. Through this mike who mars can hear what the speaker wants to say without any kind of speaker

He started speaking on it.

"Dear people of Mars, I Henry Albus is going o kill Nalmart. From now you are save from this crazy creature. I know that Nalmart is never a good person."

Hearing Henry's voice every person started gathering in the front of the palace. Henry smirked and said "Good! Everyone please come outside the palace. I know you all say that Nalmart is good person but he is never a good person. I know in your heart, you know Nalmart is not a good person. And now everyone is free from him. I am not giving you this transformigation watch because it would not be good in other people hands. So now choose your king."

Henry threw Nalmart off from the balcony. Everyone started cheering when Nalmart fell and he was dead. Henry went to the earth. He lived with his mother for days but he was very guilty about the death of his friends. His mother also died. Due to his mother's death is sister too died. His friends John lived in his own life. No one was his in the earth now. This all happened in a week. In 2 week, henry has lost his mother, Fred, James, Ella, Meonga, Geonda, Bounty, sisters and a friends. 8 deaths in 2 weeks. Henry was not able to see all these and he went on his building top. He went near the wall, climbed it and fell. He opened his hand and enjoyed while he was falling. Bang!!!

Our hero dies!

The adventure is still not finished

What happens after that?

After few years

When Henry's soul goes to GOD, God say "Henry you are a very honest and kind person. You have sacrificed your life for those people, if you wanted then you would never go there, and those people would die but you are a brave person. But my son, the earth has many more problems. There are some problems which no one knows. I am sending you back on earth. You will live there for some years and someone will come to you. He will show you the problems. Now go, go my son."

Henry obeys Jesus Christ and go to the earth back! What happen next?

Yahya Ashraf, has wrote one more book. It's name is James Cook- the fantastic adventure of James cook. Order it online on Amazon or Barnes and Noble. Simply type Yahya Ashraf. You can also call partridge India at 0008001006262 or you can read it online.

You can fan mail Yahya Ashraf at yashrafjamescook@gmail.com

Or visit www.cookjames.com. You can also follow him at yahyaashraf110 on twitter.

About the Author

Yahya Ashraf is a young author. He is just 11 years old and he has written 2 books. He live in India and study in Cambridge International School. His favorite author is J.k Rowling but he likes to read Roald dhal. J.K Rowling is his inspiration for writing books.

Some facts of Mars

- -They had a teleporting machine threw which you can teleport to anywhere
- -If you're you drop something on the road and you can find it, then you can tap thrice on the street. It will come to you.
- The aliens lived 200 years
- -The aliens also thought that if someone lived on other planet and they use to send their astronauts.
- In 2222 they found Earth
- In 2455 they found humans
- Aliens were always jealous by the looks of Humans
- The aliens didn't worshipped any one till 2000

When they started worshipping Jesus Christ

- The aliens didn't had any cast and any religion
- Aliens didn't knew anything about humans
- If you killed anyone is Mars then you will be killed at that moment
- No alien use to turn old!

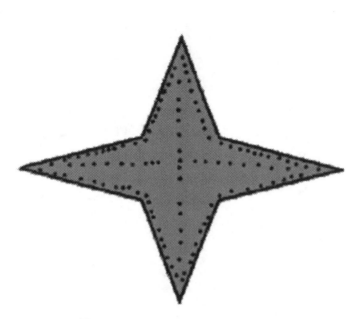

The transformigation watch

Printed in the United States
By Bookmasters